PAT HUTCHINS

The Very Worst Monster

RED FOX

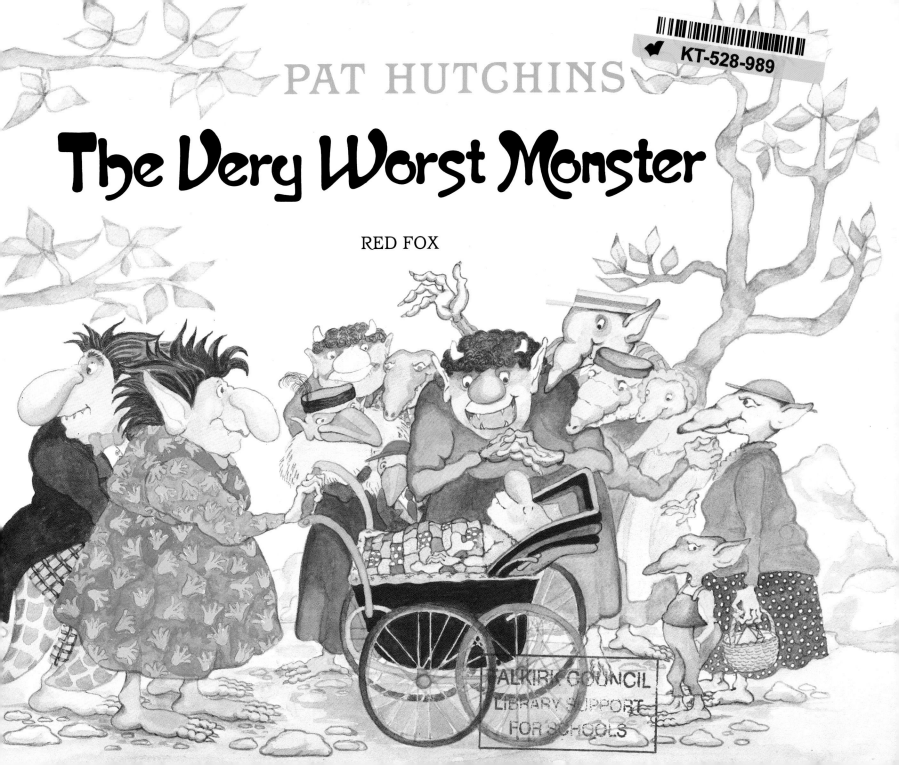

OTHER RED FOX PICTURE BOOKS BY PAT HUTCHINS

Changes, Changes · My Best Friend

Silly Billy · The Surprise Party · Tidy Titch

Tom and Sam · Where's the Baby?

The Wind Blew
(Winner of the Kate Greenaway Medal for 1974)

You'll Soon Grow Into Them, Tich

A Red Fox Book

Published by Random House Children's Books
20 Vauxhall Bridge Road, London SW1V 2SA

A division of Random House UK Ltd.
London Melbourne Sydney Auckland
Johannesburg and agencies throughout the world

Copyright © Pat Hutchins 1985
3 5 7 9 10 8 6 4

First published by The Bodley Head 1985

Red Fox edition 1996

Printed in Hong Kong

RANDOM HOUSE UK Limited Reg. No. 954009

ISBN 0 09 966041 5

The Very Worst Monster

FOR AMY

When Billy Monster was born, his pa said,
"My son is going to grow up to be
the Worst Monster in the World."

"No, he's not," said Hazel, Billy's sister.
"I am."

But nobody heard Hazel.

When Grandpa and Grandma Monster
came to visit the baby, Grandpa said,
"Look at those strong fangs!
He can bend bars with his teeth!"
"So can I," said Hazel.
But they were all so busy
watching Billy that
nobody watched Hazel.

"Listen to that noise!" said Grandma.
"He can growl already!"
"I can growl louder than that," said Hazel.
But they were all so busy listening
to Billy that nobody listened to Hazel.

"Look," said Pa. "See how he swings
on the curtains!"
"I can do that," said Hazel.
But they were all so busy looking at Billy
that nobody looked at Hazel.

"See how he scares the postman!" said Ma.

"So do I," said Hazel.

But they were all so busy admiring Billy
that nobody noticed Hazel.

Ma and Pa thought Billy was such a bad baby
that they entered him in the
"Worst Monster Baby in the World" competition.

Hazel hoped that the baby who tried
to eat the prize would win.

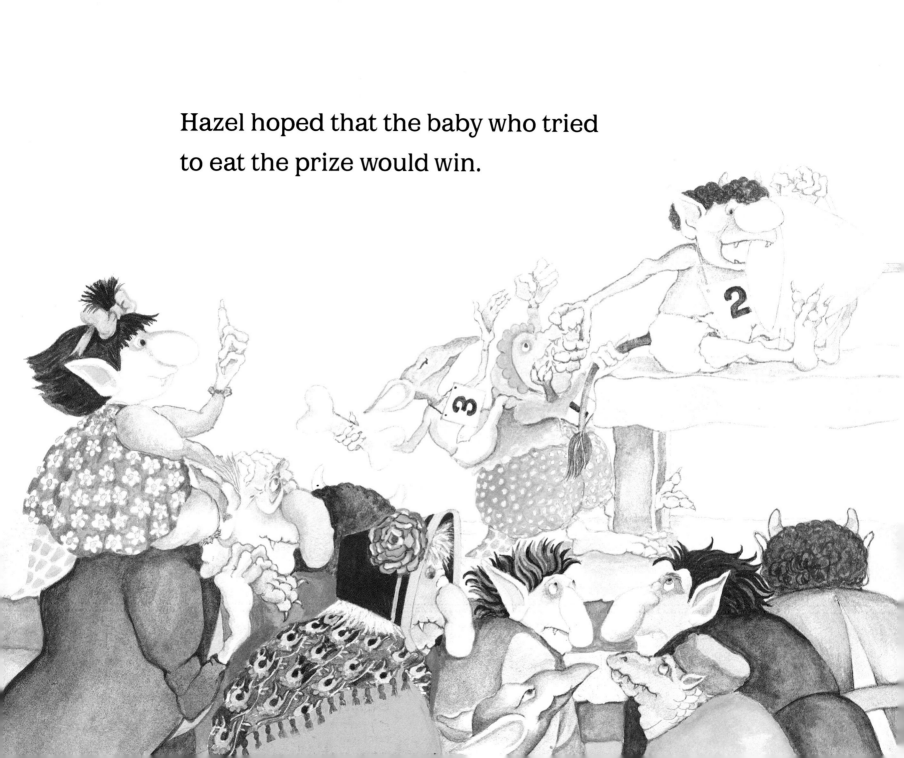

But then Billy tried to eat the judge.

"This is definitely the Worst Monster Baby in the World," said the judge.
And Billy won.

Ma and Pa and Grandma and Grandpa
were very proud of Billy.
"I know that he will grow up to be the
Worst Monster in the World,"
said Pa happily.
"No, he won't," said Hazel.
But nobody heard Hazel.

Hazel tried losing her little brother,

but he kept turning up again.

She tried frightening him away,
but that didn't work either.

So she gave him away.

"Where's Billy?" asked Ma and Pa.

"I gave him away," said Hazel.

"Oh!" cried Ma and Pa.

"You gave your own baby brother away!
You must be the Worst Monster
in the World!"

"I told you I was," said Hazel.

"I'm the Worst Monster in the World
    and HE's the Worst Baby Monster
    in the World!"
"I thought you'd given him away,"
    said Ma.

"I did," said Hazel.

"But they gave him back!"